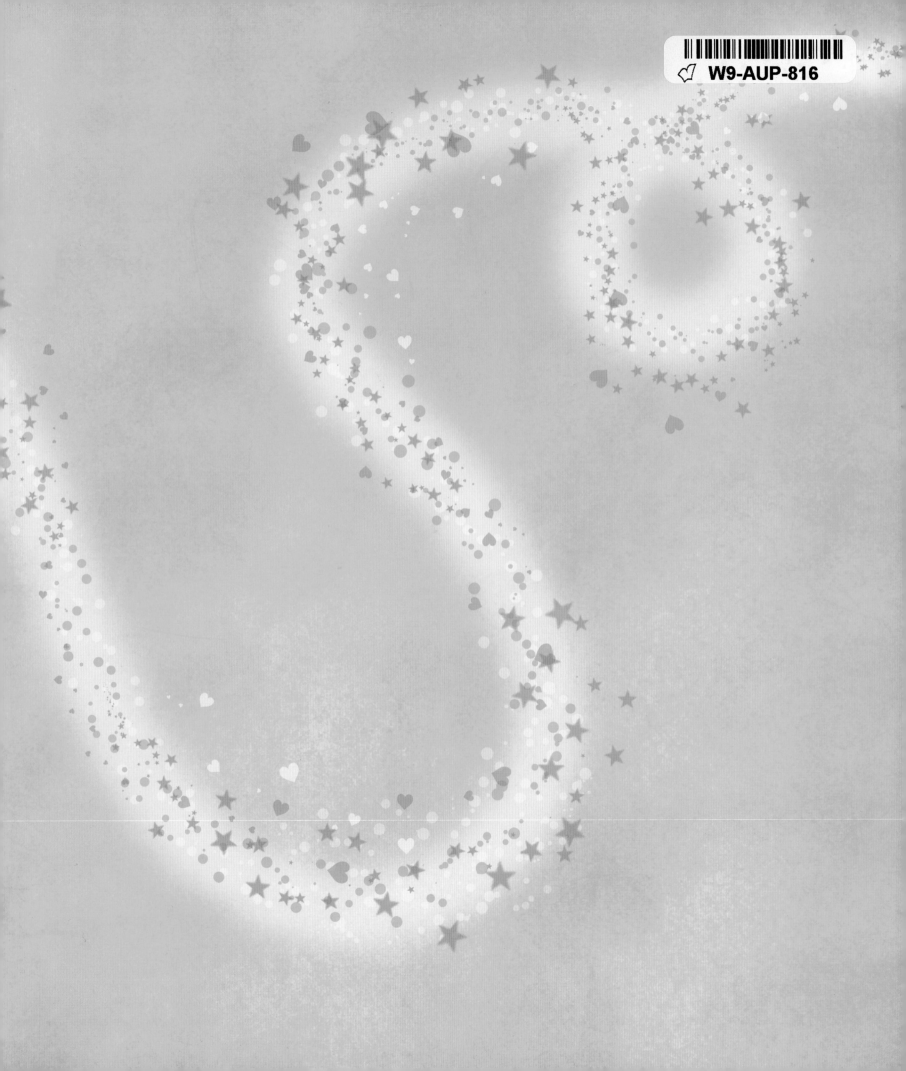

This edition published by Parragon Books Ltd in 2013 and distributed by

Parragon Inc. 440 Park Avenue South, 13th Floor, New York, NY 10016

www.parragon.com   Copyright © Parragon Books Ltd 2013

Designed by Claire Brisley and Duck Egg Blue

Edited by Lily Holland and Becky Wilson   Production by Joanne Knowlson

ISBN 978-1-4723-2912-7   Printed in China

Pinkabella

and the Fairy Goldmother

Written by
Gillian Rogerson

Illustrated by
Bruno Merz

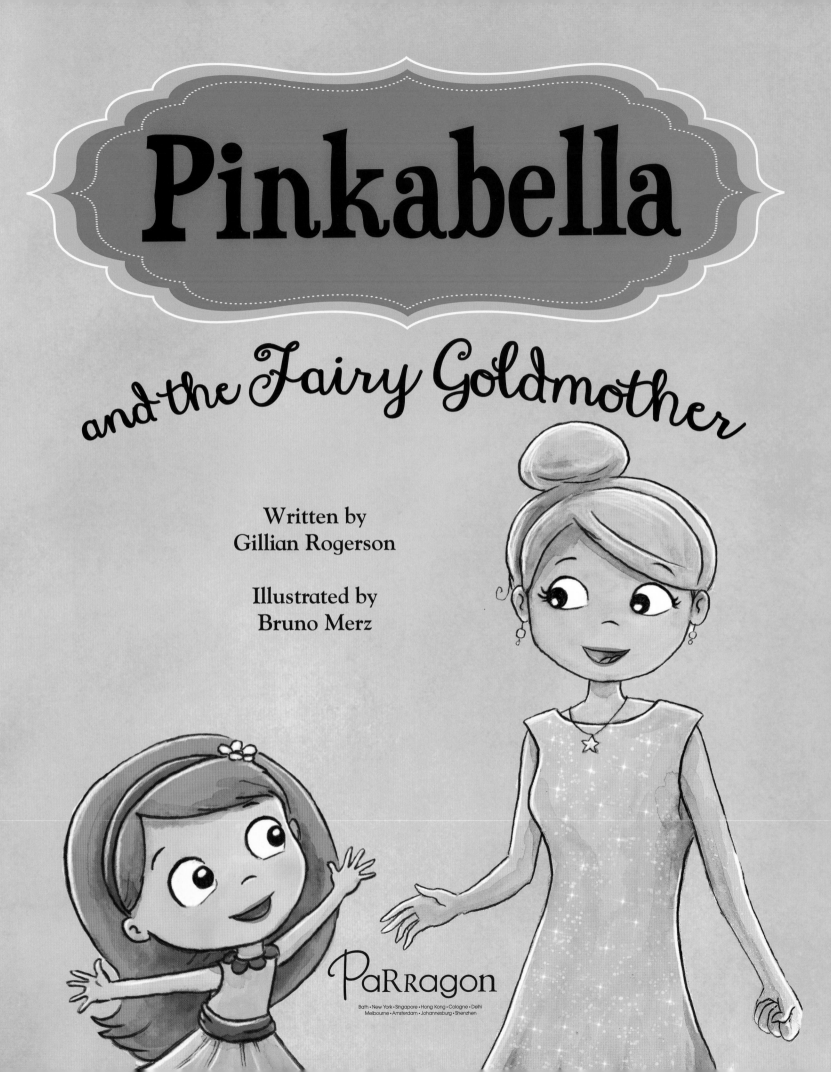

PaRragon

Bath • New York • Singapore • Hong Kong • Cologne • Delhi
Melbourne • Amsterdam • Johannesburg • Shenzhen

Pinkabella's godmother was coming to stay!
"Hello, Aunt Alura!" cried Pinkabella, excitedly. She threw
herself into her godmother's arms and nearly knocked her over.

"Whoa, steady! Now, let me look at you," Aunt Alura smiled.
"You've grown so much. Do you still think I'm your fairy
godmother?"

Pinkabella nodded and pointed to her godmother's dress.
"You're always so sparkly!"

My best friend,
Violet!

My twin brothers,
Ned and Ted!

Aunt Alura laughed. "Maybe I'm your fairy **gold**mother ...
You know I love gold almost as much as you love pink!"

"You're sleeping in my room," Pinkabella told her aunt, "and I'm staying with Ned and Ted."

"Ah, double trouble," Aunt Alura teased, reaching out to cuddle the twins.

Aunt Alura smiled when she saw Pinkabella's room, "It's very ..."

"Pinktastic!"
beamed Pinkabella.

"Pinkerrific!"
Violet added.

"Yes, and I see you've straightened up," said Aunt Alura.
"Come on, Violet," said Pinkabella. "Let's take some of my things
to Ned and Ted's room."

"Hmm," said Pinkabella,
when they got to Ned and Ted's room,
"I'm missing something ..."

My favorite
pink pj's!

Pinkabella ran back to her room and opened the door.

"Eek," she gasped in horror.

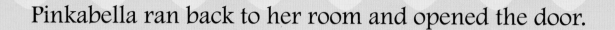

Everything in her room was *gold!*

There wasn't one bit of pink anywhere!

"My pinktacular room is gone!" cried Pinkabella.

"Aunt Alura has goldified it!"

"But how did she do that?" asked Violet. Suddenly, Pinkabella saw a sparkly stick on the end of her bed ...

"It looks like a wand," said Pinkabella.
"Do you think it's magic?" asked Violet.
Pinkabella grabbed the stick. "Let's try it!"

She waved the wand and said,

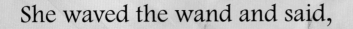

"Make everything

pinktastic!"

Suddenly, the wand made a fizzing noise,
and pink sparkles shot out of the end ...

The sparkles whizzed through the air,

and everything they landed on

turned *bright pink*.

"Wow, it IS real! Let's take turns!" said Violet, stretching out one hand.

Pinkabella threw the wand to Violet, but it whizzed over her friend's head, bounced off the wall, and zoomed back toward Pinkabella.

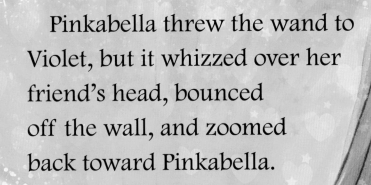

"Aargh!" cried Pinkabella, ducking down, and the wand flew out of the open window.

Pinkabella and Violet watched in horror as the wand twirled away, shooting pink sparkles everywhere it went.

Down it spiraled toward the yard ...

and Pinkabella's family!

Pinkabella and Violet ran into the yard.

"I'm really sorry, Aunt Alura!" Pinkabella began. "I didn't know your wand was real. I just wanted my room to be pink again!"

"It's okay, I'm sorry too," Aunt Alura smiled at Pinkabella. "I shouldn't have made your room gold without asking you. Now, let's get everything back to normal."

Dad smiled, "So one of you loves pink and one of you loves gold. What are you going to do?"

"I have an idea. Can I borrow your wand, Aunt Alura?" asked Pinkabella.

"Pink and gold together ... I love it!" Aunt Alura beamed.
Pinkabella twirled around.